GROWING UP

Moving

Vic Parker

Heinemann Library
Chicago, Illinois

www.heinemannraintree.com
Visit our website to find out more information about Heinemann-Raintree books.

To order:
☎ Phone 888-454-2279
💻 Visit www.heinemannraintree.com to browse our catalog and order online.

Edited by Dan Nunn, Rebecca Rissman, and Sian Smith
Designed by Joanna Hinton-Malivoire
Picture research by Elizabeth Alexander
Originated by Capstone Global Library Ltd
Printed in the United States of Amercia by Worzalla Publishing.

092011
006385RP

Library of Congress Cataloging-in-Publication Data
Parker, Victoria.
   Moving / Vic Parker.
      p. cm.—(Growing up)
   Includes bibliographical references and index.
   ISBN 978-1-4329-4800-9 (hc)—ISBN 978-1-4329-4810-8 (pb) 1. Relocation (Housing)—Juvenile literature. 2. Moving, Household—Juvenile literature. I. Title.
   HD7288.9.P37 2011
   648'.9—dc22   2010024194

Acknowledgments
We would like to thank the following for permission to reproduce photographs: Alamy pp. 6 (© Design Pics Inc.), 7 (© Image Source), 10 (© Golden Pixels LLC), 11, 13 (© Radius Images), 15 (© Glowimages RM), 17 (© Image Source), 18 (© PhotoStock-Israel), 19 (© avatra images); © Capstone Publishers Ltd pp. 8, 9. 16, 21 (Karon Dubke); Corbis pp. 23 glossary charity (© Tim Pannell); Shutterstock pp. 4, 23 glossary neighborhood (© Hannamariah), 5 (© Rob Marmion), 12 (© Christina Richards), 14 (© kRie), 20 (© Monkey Business Images), 23 glossary apartment (© haak78).

Front cover photograph of a mother and daughter moving into a new home, unpacking a cardboard box reproduced with permission of Alamy (© Beyond Fotomedia GmbH). Back cover photographs of a van reproduced with permission of Shutterstock (© Christina Richards), and boxes reproduced with permission of © Capstone Publishers (Karon Dubke).

Every effort has been made to contact copyright holders of material reproduced in this book. Any omissions will be rectified in subsequent printings if notice is given to the publisher.

Contents

Some words are shown in bold, **like this**.
You can find them in the glossary on page 23.

What Does "Moving" Mean?

People live in different types of homes.

Many people live in houses or **apartments**.

"Moving" means leaving your home and going to a new one.

You take everything that belongs to you with you.

Why Might I Move?

You might move because your family has grown bigger or smaller.

Your current home might not be the right size for your family anymore.

You might move to be closer to other family members.

You might also move because people in your family change their school or job.

How Can I Prepare for Moving?

You might feel upset at the thought of leaving your current home.

Putting photographs into a memory book might make you feel better.

Moving is a good time to go through your things and give some items away.

You could give things you do not want to **charity**, sell them, or throw them away.

What Will Happen Before Moving Day?

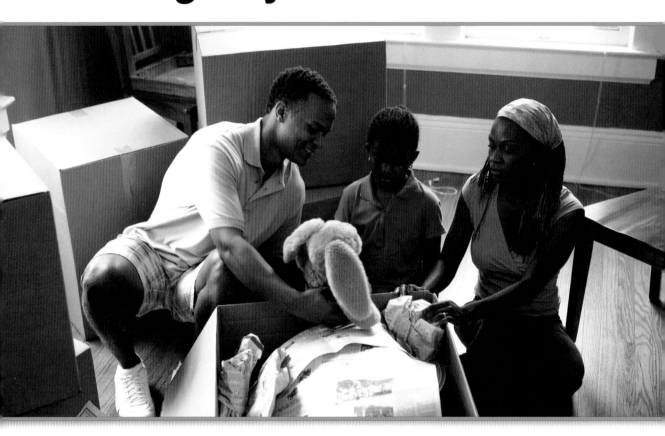

You and your family will pack up all the things that need to go with you.

Each box will be labeled, so that you know what is inside.

It is thoughtful to leave your home clean for the people who will live there next.

There will be lots of dusting, vacuuming, and polishing you can help with.

What Happens on Moving Day?

On moving day, everything you are taking with you has to be carried out.

It may all be packed into a van or truck so it can be driven to your new home.

Bit by bit, your home will be cleared of all your belongings.

Bare rooms can look, sound, and feel very strange.

How Will I Feel on Moving Day?

You may feel a little sad to leave the home you know.

Thinking about your new home might make you feel better.

However, you may feel excited on moving day.

Moving to a new home can be fun!

What Will Happen at the New House?

When you arrive at your new home, your belongings will be carried inside.

All the boxes and furniture need to be put in the right rooms.

Then you can begin unpacking and arranging your things.

It may take a while, but your new house or **apartment** will soon feel like home again.

Will I Still See My Friends?

If you move nearby, you will not be far from your friends.

You will probably be able to see them as much as you do now.

If you move to a different **neighborhood**, you can still keep in touch with friends.

You can speak on the phone or the computer, and you can visit each other.

What Other Changes Can Moving Bring?

Moving can bring many changes.

You may go to a different school or join different clubs or teams, where you can make some great new friends.

You will have new neighbors to meet.

You will also have many new places to explore, such as playgrounds, parks, and stores.

How to Help on Moving Day

Dos:

✓ Do help with the last cleaning tasks.

✓ Do keep your favorite toy in a backpack you can wear all the time, so it does not get lost.

✓ Do have a snack and a drink in your backpack, too.

Don'ts:

✗ Don't unpack packed boxes.

✗ Don't get in the way of people carrying boxes and furniture.

✗ Don't leave anything important to you lying around. It may get packed, thrown away, or lost.

Picture Glossary

 **apartment** type of home in a large building. Some buildings have many apratments in them.

 **charity** group of people who work together to help others who are in need—for instance, by selling old clothes and toys

 **neighborhood** area around your home. It includes all the streets, people, stores, schools, and parks.

Find Out More

Books

Barber, Nicola. *Moving to a New House* (The Big Day!). New York: PowerKids, 2009.

Joyce, Melanie. *A New House* (Fred Bear and Friends). Pleasantville, N.Y.: Weekly Reader, 2008.

Mayer, Cassie. *Homes* (Our Global Community). Chicago: Heinemann Library, 2007.

Websites

A website with lots of tips about moving:
http://kidshealth.org/kid/feeling/home_family/moving.html

Index